The push and pull of the sea
is an indifferent force,
a calculation of the earth entire
and of the moon....

~ *Charles D. Tarlton*

ALSO BY CHARLES D. TARLTON

Peaches and Roses – Episodes in the Navajo Degradation

Carmody and Blight – The Dialogues

Get Up and Dance

Touching Fire - *New and Selected Ekphrastic Prosimetra*

ALSO BY CHARLES D. TARLTON

LITTORAL

by

Charles D. Tarlton

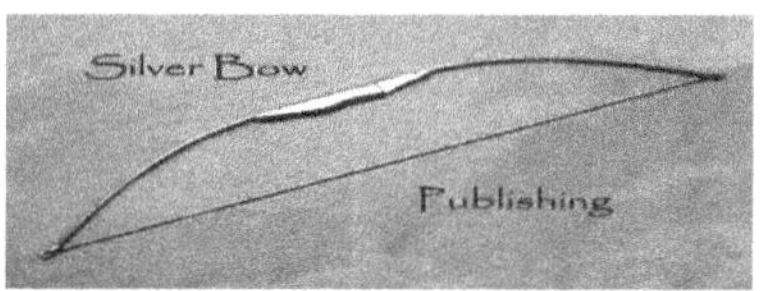

Silver Bow Publishing
720 Sixth Street, Unit # 5
New Westminster, BC
CANADA V3L3C5

Title: Littoral
Author: Charles D. Tarlton
Cover Art: "November Beach" painting by Candice James
Layout and Design: Candice James
Editor: Candice James

www.silverbowpublishing.com
info@silverbowpublishing.com
© Silver Bow Publishing 2021
9781774031797 Print
9781774031803 eBook

Library and Archives Canada Cataloguing in Publication

Title: Littoral / Charles D. Tarlton.
Names: Tarlton, Charles D., 1937- author.
Description: Poems.
Identifiers: Canadiana (print) 20210323108 | Canadiana (ebook) 20210323183 | ISBN 9781774031797
   (softcover) | ISBN 9781774031803 (Kindle)
Classification: LCC PS3620.A79 L58 2022 | DDC 811/.6—dc23

Dedication

"To Ann, my best reader."

Acknowledgements

I would like to formally credit Candice James
for lineation of the poems.

Contents

First line of each poem

1

A single sailboat moving slowly,
a little distance off the beach,
and flying only her jib,
becomes, in the dwindling bronze light,
a silhouetted, lateen-rigged felucca in an old movie
about Charlton Heston sailing somewhere up the Nile.

2

**A stone cannot fall from the sky - there ARE no stones in the sky.
~ Antoine Lavoisier**

The night sky, visible through thin low clouds,
stretched over the stony beach,
climbed the chalk cliffs,
and slid behind the hills to the south.

A windless tide lapped at the sand,
a subtle rhythm, almost mute.

It was eleven o'clock at night on the Normandy coast
near *Quiberville-sur-Mer* in 1729.
Perhaps it was the noise first, the roar and raucous hissing,
but then the light arrived, a burst of brilliance
you would have seen first muted through the clouds
and then a sudden blast of fire,
and a rain of red-hot glowing stones,
thousands of them,
that strafed the nearly flat water
and pelted the stony beach.
Almost immediately, it was over.

More than two centuries later,
American tourists complained about the rocky beach,
until just before lunch,
when one of the children found a large stone,
eight inches long and thick like a potato.

It weighed many times what it should have weighed,
and had a pimpled, virtually metallic surface.
The tourists passed the rock around, again and again,
and no one could get over its great weight.
In the *chambre d'hôte*
madame used the common little meteorites for door stops.

"Kryptonite," the eleven year old boy proposed,
"like in Superman."

3

A sentence emerges from the rock by heavy work;
you think you can think it,
how it forms its words and breaths,
but the spontaneous brain knows no stone rhythms,
it just emits.

You only harden its formation later, on reflection.
Something mechanical, then,
to count off in beats and hesitations.

Everything's like everything else logically
(yellow, for example, except for the things that aren't),
but there's always something, a tree or a rock
that, once you've named it,
becomes a special leafy hemlock
or mystical feldspar on a cave wall.

On the tide-relinquished sand,
in the coils of golden knotted sea wrack,
lay a prodigious crab.

In the fight (as I imagined it had gone)
the seaweed had been severed loose
and the crab dragged it all to shore,
where both subaqueous warriors now lay spent.

I can still recall the rush that was mine at the time...
but, Oh! This is a million miles from what I had in mind.

4

They are raking the empty beach at Hammonasset
with a John-Deere tractor,
and the memories of yesterday's sunny seaside delights,
the thousand bright beach umbrellas,
all the glistening sunbathers,
and brilliant sand castles
have all been erased.

A busload of early arrivals,
dragging their equipment toward the beach,
hesitates at the sight of the virginal sand,
so smooth and ribboned,
wondering …
if they are allowed to disrupt
the flat expanse
that stretches now
like aisles of vacuumed carpet,
or the stubble …
once the hay's been baled.

5

In the last meters of sand, wrack, and berm,
exhausted from pounding the shore with waves,
the sea expires, flattens, and slides back
into the inexhaustible blue.

The tide slides up the beach in its own time,
and there are old women
in slouchy bathing suits
sitting half on the sand
and half in the water,
as it pushes in and out
and threatens to submerge them,
to pull the sand, grain by grain,
from under them,
as if to drag their loose bosoms
and wrinkled legs out to sea.

> *The push and pull of the sea*
> *is an indifferent force,*
> *a calculation of the earth entire*
> *and of the moon as they circle each other*
> *in the airless universe.*
> *And the sun from the center*
> *looking down is burning.*

On hot summer days,
climbing down the rocky path to the beach,
I have felt the uncertainty of the sea
where it meets the sand and turns away.
There are those who say we came from the sea
and in some deep and primitive center
we long to return to it.

But that can't be the truth.
The slightest mouthful of an errant wave
or the breathing in of it
confirms we are oxygen-suckers
bound to the dry land.

6

People joke
that making hay from mahogany
is a lot like shucking gold.

> *(When I came to the window,*
> *the starlings rose up en masse*
> *from the ash tree*
> *at the edge of the marsh.)*

The day was an oppressive Maya blue in all directions,
and with the profusion of greens in the trees
it was like something made of glass
that had been sliced and layered with bright lights
all the way out to the horizon.

Of course, then, you would think about the sailboats,
which are so beautiful, with their sails taut-billowed
against the wind, leaning as they do.

> *(But then, of course,*
> *most of the sailboats would be at anchor*
> *somewhere, in a cove or harbor.)*

You wanted littler things, I know,
like the last ambiguous remark
some girl said to a boyfriend
or what it's like to sit having an espresso
all alone at Starbucks.

But listen to the wind, just listen to it!
There is a little icehouse along the road there

in Madison, Connecticut,
where they sell you ice to keep your fish cold;
it always reminds me of a little chapel
that had been turned into a house
along the road between
Calamandrana and Rocchetta Palafea.

7

A white ash in the park
was filled with black starlings.
I looked up when a bright red cardinal sailed by,
and a robin, and a ruddy house finch, all partly red,
and a wren.

The Audubon Field Guide
lists warblers and juncos, nuthatches,
titmice, and chickadees,
but there were none here to be seen.

Three blue jays, fangs out,
were mobbing a slowly moving crow
in a dogfight while,
in the distance,
high above the town.

Mocking grackles
welcome Brueghel's winter hunters
limping home empty-handed from the hunt.

8

There is a kind of crow that habituates the shore,
squawks like a gull from the top of a street light
and scavenges along the beach
for dead, cast-up fish and discarded sandwich wrappers.

We see them in amongst the herring gulls,
shiny black interlopers,
hopping and pecking at mollusks
and shrimps in the swash.

What makes a blackbird want to be a seabird?

I read somewhere that hawk-like hooks
have been found on the ends of some fish crows' bills,
perhaps the tiniest first sign of evolution toward the osprey
or Pallas's rough sea eagle.

Hippity-hoppity metamorphosis
from backshore to the berm.

9

A dark vulture was circling
over the water in the cove
while I sat waiting for Ann to come back
from her walk with the dog.

At first, I thought it had to be an osprey
because there were splayed feathers at the ends of the wings,
but I changed my mind, and said to myself,
that it really must be a vulture.

I had often watched what were unmistakably vultures
circling over roadkill on Route 9 on the way to Essex,
and I had noticed the ends of their wings were also splayed,
        like fingers —
and this bird then gliding over the cove
had those in spades.

But, just as I had finished debating with myself,
the bird suddenly dropped mid-sweep
like a proverbial stone
(I actually thought for a second he'd been shot)
and slammed into the water)
in a convulsion of foam,
came wildly clawing out,
a fallfish struggling in its talons,
and headed straight up and over the trees.

I said to myself,
not even looking around …
that was no buzzard.

10

Τερψιχόρη

A gray herring gull fights wildly
in the onshore wind, like a kite on its string,
somersaults all elbows and angular.

trees applaud and sway seductively

From where I am watching through my window,
well out of the wind, there is music playing,
something with violins.

leaves vibrate on their twigs and stems

And the gull begins deliberately to dance,
devising Isadora Duncan moves,
a barefoot bird.

feathers maneuvering toward a climax

And then he turns, and the wind lifts him from behind,
and he sails away,
skiing down the wind.

now sand dunes and waves are dancing

11

As I was walking along the path
down to the cove,
all in the same instant these events occurred —
five cormorants posed regally on five black pilings
and another on a rock;
a fish crow landed on top of an electric pole;
two herring gulls stayed at rest
on a blue-and-white ketch's furled after sail;
an osprey circled slowly higher up;
and a snowy egret,
its long neck tucked in compactly,
flew straight across the picture,
right to left,
two meters above the water,
dragging my eye with it.

In the confluence of stars,
and while I was walking along the path
leading down to the cove,
all in the same instant,
these events occurred....

12

25

You often hear about profound thinkers
from the past,
the Paris conversations in Voltaire's time
or the Tao as Lao Tzu taught it,
and I wonder if now we'd even understand them,
the world being so utterly changed since then.

For hours I watched an old man
in the library reading Kant,
and I wondered,
when we both got up to leave at closing time,
if he would go on to a different kind of world from mine.

Would he touch and smell the *ding an sich*
under the layers of estimate and error,
and know the real names of things
as yet unseen?

13

In one painting there was a hat,
easily recognized as a hat,
on the painted head of a laborer
gleaning the wide flat fields.
No cooling wind raised the long shirttails
from his back.

mystically, walls fall or turn to glass
in the wind-rippled water

In another painting,
men and women are together
in the fresh mowed fields on a hot harvest day.

Some are working,
some are resting in the shade...
but wait, go back,
what if there was no hat there at all?

Maybe only a rough smudge
of yellow and brown paint
from the end of a heavily dipped brush

miracle of reflected reflections
in the smiles of their ecstasy

making a rough, muddy ovoid,
and then they all said:

"Why, that looks nothing at all like a hat!"

14*

I waited near the canvas
until the guard was looking away
 and I was able to slip in between the women
walking under the blooming green and yellow chestnut trees
in Van Gogh's painting.

That's me there in the red dress, tagging along.
The darkness stands at bay in a wood or park corner,
and is that a cloud?
Oh, France! Oh, my beloved!
These are, let's say, patchy yellow and green painted streets
under the yellow and white flowers,
and a woman in a yellow dress
and a woman in a green dress
(green that almost disappears in the verdant growth).

Trees accumulate to fill the vision,
a cloud of green leafage swelling as if
(and were there time)
they would consume the picture.

And a green man is coming along!
He's wearing a red beret.
He could be leaving the restaurant with its many reds
(doors and gutters and chimneys)
and the women are going in that direction.

I'm eager to eat something,
so I'm hurrying along in my red dress
with the women in their yellow and green dresses,
dresses the color of the trees and the roads.

With the green man comes a story,
perhaps, of an awkward intrusion,
menacing the green and yellow French day.

Is he watching the women?
My dress is the color of the stranger's beret,
and the chimneys, of course.

*Vincent Van Gogh, *Chestnut Trees in Blossom*,
Oil on canvas, 70.0 x 58.0 cm., *Auvers-sur-Oise*: May 1890,
private collection. In the public domain.

15

From forty-thousand feet,
you see irrigator circles all over Kansas;
they look like an old-fashioned plane geometry book.

These are secrets never meant to be disclosed to us
who were not designed to fly,
these are writings on the ground for birds to read.

Anyway, the mother was certain there was something there,
a spark if nothing else.

There are children, say it straight out,
who are just not good at math.

Oh, arithmetic's more or less common sense,
but take algebra or geometry
and some minds just won't encompass it.

All you can do is memorize the patterns,
give up decoding the unknowns.
Évariste Galois made his name in polynomials,
necessary and sufficient, like a compass;
push its needle arm into the paper
and clamp the pencil just opposite,
then move the pencil around
only as far as it can from the center,
round and round in circles it goes.

We used to graze our horses
on ropes tied to the ring in their halters, on one end,
and to an old car axle pounded into the ground
with a sledge hammer, on the other.

By the end of the day
they'd gnawed a nearly perfect circle
in the grass and weeds.
Or, as my ten-year-old son remarked,
"they're like Martian landing pads."

And, lastly, this:
in Arabic the roots of algebra
come from a word meaning "bonesetter,"
someone who puts the broken parts together.

16

Here is where some word
squeezed out of the wrong tube
gives the sentence an odd *Phthalocyanine Blue* color,
resists plain meaning,
and sends your head in an indecorous direction.

Still, you can finish the thought.

You were asking about someone who died,
and I racked my brain to come up with someone.

Was that anyone you knew on the bus,
the one who was listening in,
overheard us,
and asked that same question
out of ignorance?

Was it a girl or a boy sent you into orbit
with a circle drawn around your head
as a sign of your significance or dullness?

Everyone has come in here
to hear your answers,
so what exactly was the question?

Till now it's been about love.

All this time?

Then my fingers reached for ties to bind,
for a bow from her hair, for comfort.

When, with my eyes shut,
I list the girls I've known,
You just say ...
"Nobody knows where they are now."

17

You wake into the noise
of a sudden morning,
listening but not really hearing,
like reaching for handfuls of water
from a stream.

Some distance from it now,
fainter with the wind dispersing,
making it whisper, you can hear:
"There were roses here," she said.
"Roses, near the dunes,
where the waves and backwash noises,
sea mists, and the storms were all part of it."

You could see Long Island
muted in the distance,
a long dark jabot line
with faintly hinted trees
along the horizon
and there was a slow
rough-edged black barge
going east.

18

Night concedes its domination of the sky
and, at the first hint of the sun,
like an elixir poured into wine,
threads of sunlight diffuse through the inky darkness,
thinning it, diluting it,
running it through the color wheel
from black, through purplish gray,
to sudden bleeding reds
along the far horizon's edge,
as dawn tears its way through.

Morning arrives with skies gone all pale blue.

19

Everyone I knew in high school
is either old and rich now,
or they died too young somewhere along the way.

One good friend was killed in a motorcycle crash;
a pickup truck ran into him
on the night his second daughter was born.

Another guy's Skyhawk was shot down over Hanoi.

Still a third retired early only to die almost immediately
from a pervasive cancer.

Once I realized I'd outlived nearly everybody,
I resolved to treat each day special,
you know, make up for being the one still alive.

    But the days went by so fast.

I had trouble separating that moment
when the sun was just coming up
from when it was just going down.

But hold up here.
I'm sorry,
but the guy who's been telling this story
has been shouted down.

Somebody else wants the microphone,
and the crowd's getting itchy,
so the proprietor has called for a round on the house.

A very tiny but perfectly proportioned man
tries to get everybody's attention,
but he can't reach the mic,
and he just stands there hollering his head off.

20

Nikki, the poodle, is reluctant
to move off her mat,
as all around her signs of impermanence
are thick in the air.

Books are going into boxes,
the china plates wrapped and crated,
rugs are rolled and tied,
the icebox has been emptied,
and the beds stripped.

The big orange truck pulls up
and the guys are coming in.

The dog is up at the window now,
and barking furiously.

She's not about to let this happen
on her watch.

21

The wolf,
its eyes hard and yellow on the windows,
pacing in the black and glassy-tar darkness
on soft pads, trampling the roses
and spiked blue petalous hyacinths.

*why not a dancer
landing the instant she rises - entrechat?*

Panting in loud broken rasps
and the sounds of animal spittle
as it falls in slurs on the grass,
wet insinuations on the back of my hand.

*when our bodies have perished,
what to do, then,
with all these loose, wandering, souls?*

Or , it could have been only a cough
somewhere in the house —
perhaps one of the children.

*a rat twitches his nose
and scurries underfoot
looking around for a friend.*

22

He went out into the hot fields
where Mexicans were harvesting artichokes and lettuce
in the fiery sun to the rhythm of machines.

A conveyor belt was turning in its own contraption
as it traveled down the row;
a dozen hooded workers
were tossing, tearing, chopping, packing

and he asked them about it all later, in letters,
where he put a dollar in each for an answer.

> *What do you think about*
> *out there in the sun all day?*

He imagined they would conjure thoughts of love
or home or simply resting at the end.

> *We are lucky to find work*
> *and our hearts are full.*

He made an outline in his head
where he sketched predicted answers.
The migratory worker's just like you or me, he thought.
The labors of the day give way to evening's normal joys
of family and a well-cooked meal.

And then he waited for their answers:

> *Murder,*
the first response was scrawled in the middle of the page
        in excrement.

God has forsaken us,
another sent, along with a torn-edged holy card
        of the Sacred Heart
        of Jesus as a blond.

        Thanks for the buck,
          the third one said.
        I bought a little wine.

23

In a language like ours, so many words of which are derived from other languages, there are few modes of instruction more useful or more amusing than that of accustoming young people to seek the etymology or primary meaning of the words they use. ~ **Coleridge**

Hirsute

Wild and overgrown, a terror,
something that makes your hair stand on end,
or vibrates the tiny filaments
on the undersides of leaves

I'd always thought the word was "hair-suit,"
something for Medieval penitents,
hairshirted in an uncomfortable garment
of shame and itch.

You could call it fur,
how it fills in the skin of forehead, cheeks, and chin—
Lon Chaney metamorphosing, in time lapse,
into the Wolfman.

Where the boundaries of the civilized world
were drawn by the plow,
where the land was either wild, hirsute
      (on one side)
or smooth and cultivated
      (on the other),
orderly rows of corn or the barbarous weeds.

Epizeuxis

Grown men making their reputations
by noticing tiny differences and similarities
among a billion kinds of moths:

Epizeuxis Hübner, 1818 was referred from the Herminiinae
to the Hypeninae within the Noctuidae by Tikhomirov, 1979,
Trudy Zoologicheskogo Instituta Akademii Nauk SSSR 82 : 88.
Poole (1989) included EPIZEUXIS Hübner, 1818;

CAMPTYLOCHILA Stephens, 1834;
HELIA Duponchel, 1845 (preoccupied);
CAMPYLOCHILA Agassiz, 1847;
HELIA Guenée, 1854 (preoccupied);
PSEUDAGLOSSA Grote, 1874;
and ZENOMIA Dognin, 1914
as junior synonyms of IDIA Hübner, 1813.

But, its true domain was rhetoric!
From the Greek, repeat the Greek, the Greek, the Greek,
noticing reiteration's drumbeat,
hammering a bell to get your attention.

I came upon two butterflies on an orchid,
pale and tangerine, brilliant moths,
a church window of color in their wings,
one, two, one, two, the same to my eye, identical.
They fanned the air slowly
like Utamaro Geishas gently, lest they fly,
and at the last minute,
I saw the quick diaphanous wings move:
on the one, a startling red DIAMOND,
where the other wore the MOON, the MOON! the Moon!

Belliferous

Oh, what a beautiful (bellus) war (bellum),
and they say he was a rather good fighter.
And I patiently soothe my anger,
retire, and let better feelings intervene.
Bells! Bells!

And the pumping hot bellows,
the red hot tip of horseshoe.
Watch the organ's bellows,
the organist is pumping out a rage.

Sometimes,
the words encircling one another,
the bells peel.
And the toughest haul is to begin again,
to pick up the old battle,
a way of saying war, battle, death,
and hand-to-hand combat,
but in the Latinate to dull the edge,
once sharpening the blade;
did the war-eagle know?

Did the fudging in the foreign language assuage?
Can you say, even say, belliferous
and not feel deeply patrician?
A noble word, belliferous,
(not a common word, not combative or quarrelsome)
keep "bellicose" and "belligerent"
for St. Crispin's Day speeches,
oratorial dirges and eulogies —

Ah, Belliferous, my son.

24*

**"...*a train is an extraordinary bundle of relations because it is
something through which one goes, it is also something by means of
which one can go from one point to another, and then it is also
something that goes by.*" ~ Michel Foucault**

There's me, you and the train;
the train, me, and you.
I am not the train.
I am only walking through the train,
to the dining car, perhaps,
or back to my seat.

The train is passing through Mullingar
on its way from Dublin to Sligo.

You are a lorry driver
stopped at a crossing in Mullingar
and watching the train go by.
You are in a hurry and somewhat annoyed.
I am having tea in the lounge car and, looking out,
I see you, but barely,
because you are going by so quickly.

The dancer is curled up on the floor,
his right arm reaches out ahead,
curls back under the small of his own back,
then thrusts suddenly out!
The movements fade into the memory
as fast as they rise to consciousness,
a flow just like a movie,
there and gone,

around the stage like a Chinese dragon
dragging its tail in a parade.

Did you see me looking out?
Did you see me wave?
I was sitting and having tea
and looking out at you, and waving.
All the time I was moving from Dublin toward Sligo.
Dublin was sliding away, forgotten;
Sligo was waiting.
You were gone then behind the moving trees and rooftops,
and its took me a little less than a mile to finish my tea.

Dance's penmanship's revealed
as arms and legs write in the air, across the floor.
There's no message, though,
just traces from the dancer and the dance.

The dancer approaches, leaps, and turns in flight,
describing unforeseen marks
faster than the human eye can connect them up.
He dances along a path so quickly taken up
it's already a memory,
an ethereal scaffolding of unseen, unheard of forms.
Vocabularies from ballet, some feel,
inscribe common experiences; you can read, they say,
an arabesque, fouetté or cabriole.

The dancer's stockinged feet leap
and crisscross each other in a stutter of positions,
an e.e. cummings of the dance!
We see things quicker than we can hear them,
think them even quicker than that,
know things hitherto unknown,
and grasp the nothing, all at once.

The dance dissociates, though,
in the frames of the film,
each one captures but a portion
to make an illusion of movements we can number.

Otherwise, there is only our memory of the dancer
having moved, leaped, turned, dropped, and flown.
He set out to sketch spontaneous movement,
rode the moment's unrehearsed, untraceable lines
and squiggles** along the lake's edges
where white winter winds had blown up
something like a surf that froze mid-air,
the water piled upon itself in sculptures of pure motion.

** This poem appeared in a somewhat different form in KYSOFlash, #12, Summer, 2019. The performance, "Heterotopia" by Eldad Ben Sasson can be viewed at: https://vimeo.com/142496929. Not to be confused with the more elaborate and famous production of "Heterotopia" by William Forsythe, which can be viewed at: https://www.youtube.com/watch?v=hDTu7jF_EwY*

*** Figure 6: Sketch of 'Loss of Small Detail' (1991) from William Forsythe's notebook circa 1990, William Forsythe. From: "Dancing and Drawing, Choreography and Architecture," Steven Spier, Journal of architecture, vol. 10, no. 4, 2005 September, p.356.*

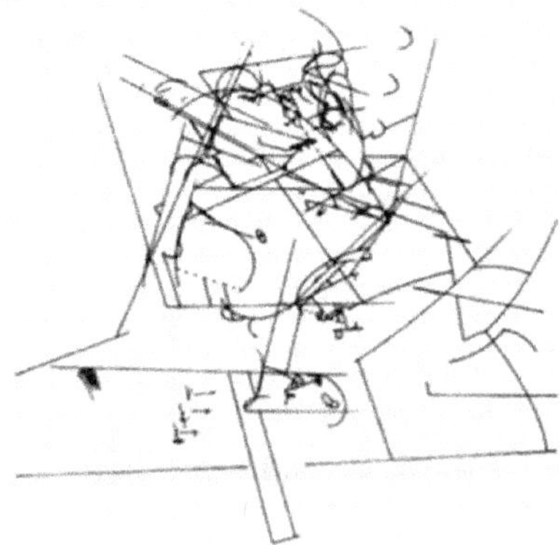

25

***a shower
of white fire!***

— Mary Oliver

Within the sense of white things,
what a snowy egret knows
beyond the muddy marsh and green reeds
come to shore
is herself reflected all in white,
a mirroring, a blinding white
that shadows unsuspecting little things.

> *white bird,*
> *white like Easter is white*

We can imagine egrets on their spindly legs
spearing fishes, insects, frogs, and snakes,
but who wears the egret's feathers anymore?
Egrets only in the moment,
watched for meaning and a beauty
hard to get your words around.

> *white bird*
> *symbolic of polished things*

The snowy egret's shadow
skates unseen across the moon's face,
a white rainbow.
On a straight line parallel with the road
across the marsh another egret flies,

her long legs stretched behind
like Baryshnikov doing high cabrioles
in La Bayadere.

    a white arrow
    shot along the treetops

From the bank of North Cove
looking across the yacht anchorage
to hills still more distant and then the railway,
one egret flies east, going left to right,
a silent white speck in the distance;
here in the foreground another fishes for minnows.

    the surface of the river
        is calm,
    reflecting everything

Just skin-deep,
our perfect beauty swallows a whole fish,
the sea behind a white thread on a nimble needle
pulled quickly through warp and woof,
a greenly sunlit picket fence of feathery reed
flowers growing in the calm salt marsh.

    phragmites australis
     choking the inlet,
    blocking our way

The snowy egret's faster than the will-o'-the-wisps.
"Athena threw an egret down the dark,"
Homer said, down in the summer salt shallows.
A bright white, alabaster statue,
under brilliant light,
outside in the glazing sun.

> *what, then,*
> *the old man wondered,*
> *is the egret, then, to me?*

A sentinel standing on an edge of sand or marsh,
so still, pure white, and stylish,
You can know more easily
the black crow caw-cawing in its treetop
or the felon gull strutting around on the sand.
But, from the egret we expect suavity, aplomb,
a perfect bird on show.

> *Two egrets*
> *like alien punctuation marks*
> *in some indecipherable writing*

What's all this to me – late sunset
reflecting red-orange off the egret's feathers,
the edge a crochet of flames,
the last light to go out,
where does the egret sleep?

> *"Dozing egrets*
> *and gulls on the sand,*
> *do not so much as turn their heads"*

Li Qingzhao, looking up
from reading the mysterious ginkgo leaves.
Rows of egrets on the wet sand dozing with gulls,
admiring lotus and sagisō (white-egret flower)
with their wispy wing feathers, like the egret
clumsy in full passion resurrected.

26

Maybe it's time to slip that osprey bone under my skin.
~ David Gessner, Return of the Osprey

Two kites have bolted Look!
from their long strings and wheel
now like acrobats on the rising air;
a vision driven in a slow regime, unrhymed,
a circumstance made to wheel
beyond our hearing's reach,
silencing poetry in its slow circles.

From Kelsey Point to Duck Island,
hanging like amulets in the sky
above Long Island Sound,
two ospreys reconnoiter the beach.
Raptors of the ocean sea.

I don't know how humanity stands it
with a painted paradise at the end of it.

~ Ezra Pound, The Pisan Cantos

Pandion haliaetus, deadpan spherule eyes
intent only on slippery fish shapes
swimming just below the ripples,
their cold yellow eyes blot out reflections
and see through to shimmering scales
from sixty feet high and on the move,
looking straight through water
like a slide under a microscope.

wedding dancers round and round
the light's illuminated surfaces,
the flat of their cheeks, their brows

Tereus, made osprey,
pursued Pandion's daughters forever.

Here!
These Osprey soaring high and silently on rising air,
on glider's wings, became salt-river's stealthy terror,
decoding this simple feathered impetus
sent from their medulla: fish!

Heedless menhaden roar up
in a wild froth in clenchèd talons,
a jungle's flying fish,
"en voiture, Simone."

At the very top of the tallest mast
in North Cove sailboat harbor,
a dark and silent osprey sits
like the carved statue of a frightening owl.

"How long has he been there?" Ann asked,
as he dropped like the shadow of a stone,
feet first into the river
that was running upstream with the tide,
entered the water in a convulsion of white foam,
struggled up, clawing out of the swirl,
and displayed a silver fish.

I thinke he'l be to Rome
As is the Aspray to the Fish.

Coriolanus (1623) iv. vii. 34

The Osprey, skating on air,
moved beyond my ambit, flew away without emotion,
slowed in curves and moving circles,
freed to converse with himself,
not counting on my powers of telepathy (an easy conjure)
where I could read his mind.

> *Now high up on a long slow loop of clear sky,*
> *from where I can see twenty miles*
> *of the windy blue, stretched lines*
> *of Long Island trees,*
> *shallows under a high running tide*
> *where the bright fish are dancing.*

Then, as the osprey's eye
traced along the tilting horizon's parabolas,
far away and echoing
lines of ocean swells
arranged their odd angles;
the west wind,
the wind on which the osprey hung
as he composed this thought,

> *A wire of instinctive steel*
> *is fastened around my neck*
> *welded at the other end*
> *to the fledglings in the nest.*
> *I fly out so very far, driven,*
> *whipped by the fishing*
> *like an ache beyond my reach.*

Osprey were then everywhere;
in the red-tinted dusk
I saw one from the corner of my eye.
He was big, jointed,

and dark against pink and gray clouds,
an express letter on his way someplace.
The elbows in his flapping wings
were the giveaway;
he was here one moment,
but gone the next.

> *Out and back I come and go,*
> *out and back, a feathered metronome*
> *counting circles endlessly.*
> *Like a kite on a string,*
> *I am held up by the onshore wind,*
> *feathering the air*
> *the compass for my surveilling orbits.*

On Route 9, coming back from Massachusetts,
an osprey skimmed the treetops
running just ahead, as if guiding the car someplace,
and later a pair in overlapping circled patterns
scoured miles of reedy marshland,
driven on, always hunting, forever!

> *What I think, it's more patience than anything.*
> *Oh, and the wind. It was the tag-end of a cyclone,*
> *tearing limbs from the trees,*
> *blew all us birds off our wings,*
> *made hatchlings tremble*
> *with fear they'd be blown away.*
> *And the rain, unceasing,*
> *drowns the highest nest.*
> *To get those eggs laid,*
> *to find food for a family,*
> *fend off Racoons and Crows.*

> *Life is hard.*

27

Both my right knee and ankle
are fragile again this morning.

As long as I stay in bed I feel normal,
but as soon as I stand up
the twinges in those two joints
remind me to be careful and go slow.

I talk to myself this way;
my enduring and constant self
warns my temporary and aging self,
and we feel the impatience of death
loafing nearby, out of sight.

I envy the clear lamp-base filled with sea glass
standing atop my antique Chinese writing chest.
They are disdainful of my whimpering;
alive or dead is not a distinction they worry much about.

why do you moan so and complain?
Is there another world you'd prefer to live in?

28

~ homage to Marianne Moore

*"It cannot...be expected that the history of...Kennebunkport
can contain much matter of interest...."**

At low tide,
three red and gray Whitehall rowboats
high and dry on the Kennebunkport harbor's mud,
while three facsimile red and gray painted rowboats
float on a downtown gallery wall.

Oversized and stuffed,
a stripèd black seabass poses
frozen over the bar in Fox's,
but the painted fish fossil
(or is it a fish only half eaten?)
by Kahlil G. Gibran
hangs equally odorless
in the Museum of American Art.

Nothing ever really changes.

*Bartholomew Gosnold, *History of Kennebunk Port:
From Its First Discovery* (May 14, 1602, to A.D. 1837).

29

*I had three encouragements—1st, a smooth, calm sea; 2ndly, the tide rising,
and setting in to the shore; 3rdly, what little wind there was blew me towards
the land.* ~ **Daniel Defoe,** *Robinson Crusoe*

My line of sight
stretches from our back porch
out to the Sound, and then bends
where the marsh in May is turning green,
                             and over the marsh
to a lacey scrim of surf right-angled to my line.

> *you'd never be able*
> *to sing any of this*
> *there are blue blossoms*
> *on the Lilac bush*

Even up close, the sea stays that far away.
Its mysteries are older than almost anything.
Most of it lies underneath
the often wild surface
and it's the wind that kicks it up.

The depths are very still, dark, and cold.

> *a frantic house wren*
> *caught by its own claws*
> *in the window screen*
> *his life before his eyes*

The waves rise up in the wind,
come onto shore

and shatter against the rocks,
their white fingers clawing at the sky.
They've been sent in here
from long distances by the wind,
from far out to sea,
where it makes swells as big as hills.

> *in the time we've been here,*
> *all the leaves*
> *have come out on the trees*
> *is how shade is made*

No one here ever sits on the shore
and turns their back to the sea.

> *a cormorant's as black*
> *as the rock he waits on*
> *low tide reveals the smell*
> *of uncovered molluscs*

30

A long-necked, pure white snowy egret
slow dancing in the salty shallows,
a murderous beauty,
supple as a French curve,
its sinister beak poised for a sudden strike

> *dark clouds close in*
> *over the Sound*
> *and a blast of lightning*

that's in and out of the shallows in the same instant,
with a nameless gray crustacean dangling,
the serpentine throat urbanely convulsive
in its waves of swallowing.

> *the tide rises steadily*
> *to engulf the foreshortened shore*

The egret, on another plane is, toward us,
as insouciant as to the rocks,
to the sandy rise of the beach,
or to the distant catboat
threading its way
between channel buoys.

> *purple martins contort*
> *on the wing in the rising storm*

As our hubris encompasses everything, in our view
this egret's not so awfully unlike
the flowering beach roses
or clumps of green sea moss atop exposèd rocks,

images painted on separate panes of glass
to define dimension

we just assume things so beautiful
have been put here as attributes of our world,
among its vistas and curiosities,
delights we rightfully consume
like daylight or the air.

penniless,
he was forced to gorge
on natural beauty.

31

Her art hangs suspended on the end of a thin thread,
and two osprey come up fast above the cove
and do their curvilinear dance in the air,
turning and diving in perfect synchrony.

      Abruptly, the pursuer has peeled
off, as if he'd never really cared,
and he's gone; and then we realize
the first osprey is carrying a fish, as they do,
like a torpedo under the fuselage.

Two styles, three, a fourth, and then a fifth
sequential on the walls, squeezing
one another—a landscape with marshes,
then a twisted rose, bright colored chintz
like the face of a fuchsia and turquoise
microchip,
      and a dead horse in a field.
The promised storm continues to blow,
with thunder and storm-force winds,
and a hard cold rain is raining
in front of the Sound's obscured horizon.

32

On a darkening Sunday afternoon
in *Oltrarno Firenze* in the rain,
a variegated parrot scurrying up and down
a painted pipe that reached three floors
up and down, *fuori dalla finestra.**

Up and down he clawed, one foot chained
to the pipe like a handcuff, up and down
talking in Italian all whole while.
"Buttiamo tutto!" He squawked.
*"Esci dalla mia vita!" "Esci dalla mia vita!"***

*outside the window
**throw everything! Get out of my life!

33

Sins of an afternoon
begun out in rain and shadows
as far as one could see,
              almost still sails inching
along the horizon and "I swear,"
he said, "you can count individual trees
along the silhouette of Long Island."

On a summer afternoon
right after a thunderstorm,
and the whole world wet and shining
              as the colors in a Winsor & Newton
watercolor set,
                cadmium Yellow and Scarlett,
Crimson and burnt Umber, sap Green
and the White, Chinese. Oh, Cerulean Blue.

And someone on the radio was arguing
the virtues of the modern poem,
                saying (I swear) if it didn't scan,
it wasn't a poem. And I heard Walt Whitman
turning over among stray wheat stalks
on the side of the road, uttering
a long sigh, but a loving one.

* to appear in *The Journal (UK)*.

34

A salt fleury blew in the lee of the wind
and the sails made their obtuse triangles
lean in the blow
                      on the Bermuda-rigged sloop.
Two old lobster buoys hung off the porch railings,
gladly away from the cruel sea,
their peeling paint a lifeless reminder.
The air was very wet here, the trees turned a rich green
and leaned into the wind, and the moment waited.
Were you there?
There is so much I can't remember clearly;
did the old woman stay out on the porch
in the same wind that pushed the sails over
and made the trees dance?
And did the faded buoys reveal their terror
of the sea? I always sense in moments like these
the possibility of richer truths,
as if the universe were teasing us. Questions
hang from the sky like the buoys
on ropes from the porch, and the sun slipping
among the clouds
throws minute by minute
                      a muted light on things.

35

"de Kooning after Soutine"

The day itself, my sentiments,
                    and the song entire
struggled in my head to form themselves
into a single weathered vermillion rose,
with two or three petals missing,
surely sadder now but wiser.
                        The winter here,
the summer there, all at the same time
on a whirling sphere. The old woman leaned in
closer to the canvas, a bewildering Solomon Grundy,
looking to hang her umbrella on something.

And the sun found a hole in the clouds
its own exact size to peer through,
the edges of the ruffled burning cloud
like the wrinkling light on the fringe of the rose.

36

Here, the darkened cormorant
a blue-black plungèd submarine,
there, an imperial black *Reichsadler* drying on a rock;
and out there black Bell *Airacobras*
fly *en echelon,* half a foot over the sea.

Diving, he becomes a fish weaving through kelp,
temporary terror of the deep.

37

Starlings queue on the limbs
of a leafless winter tree
like obsidian ornaments;
small birds whose feathers
have a rainbow sheen, like oil
on water.

Starlings on the barren
branch of an October elm
along the highway.
                    Magical birds!

Who remembers, now, the sound
starlings make when lined up
there on a black leafless tree.

Light Vessels

The sea desires deep hulls—
It swells and rolls. ~ Hemingway

At the west end of Willard Bay in Old Saybrook, Connecticut,
the road turns away from the seafront,
but you can make your way on side streets
out to Cornfield Point where the old beach-stone
Hartlands mansion faces out to sea.
Some distance off the point is a buoy
warning of the shallow shoals that pose a danger to boats.
It also recalls the spot where, in 1919,
the U.S. Lighthouse Service's Light Vessel LV-51
was struck by a Standard Oil barge
and sank in eight minutes, though her crew got off safely.
Among the many ships lost around the world in 1919,
the sinking of this light vessel might seem unimportant;
it was not an act of war, no lives were lost,
and LV-51 was a small ship.

The red-painted *Light Vessel 51* was wildly sinking
on a sunny afternoon in April 1919,
after her hull was stoved in the iron nose
of a wandering oil barge.

The wreck is upright and down slightly by the bow,
settled into the monochromatic depths of the Sound.
The forward 15-20 feet of the bow
are buried in an underwater sand dune.

The rounded edges now of capstan, gunwale, and hawser
seem to sway in a gentle scour of loose sand,
blurred in the depth's silent, thick, living opacity.

Imagine now an antique Mitchell movie camera,
mounted on a boom, rising slowly up from the shingle,
backing over *Ye Castle Inn*, capturing the scene.

A mock-medieval castle made from local stones,
with an orange roof, the big hotel commands
a vista off the point. Picture, then, in 1929,
Otto Lindbergh out on his porch
stunned by the sight and sounds
of the *Light Ship* going down,
the titanic hissing as the boilers burst
and the fires went out.

Gardiner and perhaps 18 men, women and children
arrived at the mouth of the Connecticut River
in November 1635. He completed the fort at Saybrook Point
the following summer and built a windmill to grind corn
the colonists had planted that spring
at the place he called Cornfield Point.

A Puritan farmer,
looking up from hoeing the corn rows,
has heard something odd.
Over the tops of the silk-tasseled ears,
a sound like metal plates grinding.

Two *Nehantucket* women
who were levelling brush
and planting squash, beans, and pumpkin seeds,
heard the noise, and cried,
"*W'hilô,* someone's being killed!"

Like dry straws or torn branchlets of leaves
blown along in the wind, first and last up
thrown down together,
past and present mixed,
the crash and shudder
of a sunken *Light Vessel*
heard above tinkling glasses in a hotel bar,
the rasping of an iron plow
through a virgin Puritan cornfield

over the rhythmic chanting
kipunumuwôk (harvest)
of an extended American genesis,
an origin sent tumbling along
into an expanding present instant.

Paul Grazioli presented the Board with details
of a conflict he and his wife are having with a neighbor
concerning alleged obstruction of their water view
by excessively high shrubs.
He questioned what mediation steps
the Cornfield Point Association Board could take
on their behalf concerning this conflict.
He also reported that the attorneys for both sides
are involved after failed attempts to resolve this issue
"neighbor to neighbor".

You can thread events through time
like plain steel rods
through an antique hand-turned tap and die,
making opposites, or making everything the same.

It has been dark in the hold of *Light Vessel 51*
for more than a hundred years,
dark without the gimbal-hinged lights on deck,
they have so long been out.

A slow, darkly-dreamed *Flying Dutchman, LV-51*
sails on … silent, dark, and still,
bent in the bow by the tides
and the slow swaying dance of eelgrass.

The sea-bed's harvest of field and cobble stones,
rounded in slow geologic time,
dragged ashore and made into walls
and one hexagonal crenellated tower
blurs further the line between sunken and afloat.

All over New England, walls now in woods
testify to fields once reclaimed,
the bottom of the sea;
the sea-bed where *Light Vessel 51* lies,
the masonry of the local castle,
field-stone fences made clearing the fields,
the tumble-down piles along the highway.
You cannot see the *Light Vessel* under the sea;
it is too dark and deep, nor can you hear the voices
of Puritan children in the cornfield.
If you had been strolling along the seawall,
you might have seen the neighbors
squabbling over hedges and views,
though, insensible to ghostly wreckage under the sea.

Charles D. Tarlton Profile

The author is a retired politics professor from California and New York who grew up in the Southwest enamored of the sights and scents of the desert, who has always been sad that he missed the heyday of the frontier. Poetry has always been central in his life, even as he pursued a career and a living teaching political ideas. In recent years he has focused almost entirely on writing poems, however, giving him the opportunity to compile a second résumé.

He lives on the shore, now, in Connecticut, with his wife, Ann Knickerbocker, an abstract painter, and Nikki, their black standard poodle.

9 781774 031797